KLaSKY CSUPO INC.

Based on the TV series *Rugrats*® created by Arlene Klasky, Gabor Csupo, and Paul Germain as seen on NICKELODEON®

SIMON SPOTLIGHT
An imprint of Simon & Schuster Children's Publishing Division
1230 Avenue of the Americas
New York, NY 10020

Manufactured in the United States of America

This edition published by Grolier Books.
Grolier Books is a division of Grolier Enterprises, Inc.

ISBN 0-7172-8912-5

By Becky Gold
Illustrated by Sergio Cuan

Tommy Pickles was excited.
He jumped up and down.
His dad had made
the best new car!

Chuckie came over.
"What's that, Tommy?" he asked.
"It's our new car," Tommy said proudly. "It's called a cramper."

WATCH YOUR STEP

“Hey, kids,” said Stu.
“Let me give you the grand tour!”
He carried the babies
into the camper.
Inside, there was a kitchen.
There were beds that could disappear.
There was a place to play.
And there was . . . Angelica!

"So kids, ready to go camping?" asked Stu.

"Did you hear that, Chuckie?" Tommy asked. "We're gonna go camping!"

"I don't know if that's a good idea," said Chuckie.

"Look over here!" shouted Angelica. "A Safari Cynthia play set!"

"I guess Angelica is coming, too," said Tommy.

Everyone piled into the camper. Didi passed the rice cakes. Grandpa Lou shook his head.

"No chocolate," he said. "You call this a cake? Why, in my day . . ."

At last they were off!

"Tommy," whispered Chuckie, "does cramping hurt?"

Angelica heard him.
"It's *camping,* not cramping," she said.
"You know, ghost stories, wolves,
vampires—"

"GHOST STORIES? WOLVES? VAMPIRES?" Chuckie yelled.

"Don't worry, Chuckie," said Tommy. "There won't be any ghost stories or wolves."

“And a vampire is just something you roast marshmallows over.”

“Oh,” said Chuckie.

But he was still a little afraid.

Soon they arrived at the campsite.
Stu and Didi made dinner.
Grandpa Lou took Angelica, Tommy, and
Chuckie down to the lake.

“Okay, sprouts, we’re gonna catch a big fish!” Grandpa said.

“Those waves look kinda high,” Chuckie said to Tommy.

"Stroke, babies, stroke!" cried Angelica. Tommy and Chuckie rowed hard.

"Cramping is hard work," Chuckie said.

Suddenly Grandpa Lou yelled, "Stop! Here's a good fishing spot."

They waited for Grandpa Lou to catch a fish.

They waited and waited.

Finally, Grandpa Lou felt a tug on his line. "It's a big one, sprouts!" he cried.

"About time," mumbled Angelica.

Grandpa Lou caught the fish. It was huge!

"I don't like that big eyeball!" Chuckie cried. "It's staring at me!"

"The fish is not gonna bite," said Grandpa Lou.

"What do we do with it?" asked Chuckie.

"Eat it, sprout," Grandpa Lou said.

Back in the camper,
dinner was done.
Too done!
"Oh, no," said Stu.

EJECT
JUST COOK
TURBO COOK

Stu and Didi ran outside just as Grandpa Lou and the babies came back.

"Dinner's ruined," Stu said.

“No problem,” said Grandpa Lou. “There’s plenty of fish for everyone. Let’s make a campfire!”

“Not the vampire!” Chuckie groaned. But he helped collect sticks, anyway.

"There's nothing like fresh fish," said Stu.

"Ya know, Tommy?" Chuckie whispered.

"I'm not afraid of vampires anymore. They're sorta sparkly."

Tommy nodded.

"What's for dessert?" asked Angelica.

“Marshmallows!” Tommy shouted.
“Yummy!” cried Angelica.
“Mmmpfh,” said Chuckie as he smiled a big white gooey smile.
This was the best part of cramping!

Rugrats™
YUKS
-n-
STUFF

Chuckie's Guide to Monsters

There's nothing to fear but monsters.
I know, 'cause I'm an expert.
And monsters are everywhere!

It's probably a monster if:

- It moves in the dark
- It's breathing under your bed
- It growls—unless it's Spike
- Tommy wants to go look at it
- Angelica tells you it's not a monster (then it's definitely a monster!)
- It's big as a house—unless it's a house

And if it's got scales, claws, horns, wings, four tails, and six heads, it's definitely a monster.

Words From the Wise

"We're babies! We're supposed to get in trouble! That's our job!"

"You know, sometim[es] I think playing with Angelica might not be as much fun as she says it is."

"There's no 'splaining grown-ups."

"A friend is a person who does whatever you say, no matter what, and doesn't make a big deal about it."

"Eat it first, ask questions later!"

Joke Break!

Why did Reptar get a ticket?

He ran through a stomp sign.

What do you get if you cross Tommy's dad with a cow?

Beef Stu.

What do fish use to calm their babies?

A bassifier.

What do baby cats wear?

Diapurrs.

What do you get if you cross a teething ring with a chicken?

A pacifryer.

How did the Reptar wagon feel after it got new wheels?

Tired.

What do dinosaurs put on their fish sandwiches?

Reptartar sauce.

What did the lost calf say to the baby?

"I want my mooommy!"

Who would Tommy's cousin be if she'd been raised by apes?

Tarzangelica.

Why did Angelica dump beetles and worms on Tommy?

She wanted to make a baby buggy.

Advice from the Awesome Angelica

I know just how to get babies to listen to me and do things my way. So, LISTEN UP!

- Remind them that they're just dumb babies and you're a grown-up.
- Split them up by making them mad at each other.
- Bribe them with cookies and Reptar Bars (then keep the goodies for yourself, of course).

- Tell them you're a real princess, so they have to do what you say.
- Tell them you're going to dump buckets of sand on their heads if they don't do what you say.

(WARNING: Do not try Angelica's methods without permission from grown-ups!)

How to Tell Lil and Phil Apart

Lil

(Full name ends in "ian"

Bow in her hair

High chirpy voice

Wears a dressie

Pink shoes

For one day, tried acting like Angelica

Phil

(Full name ends in "ip")

No bow

Low growly voice

Wears shorts

Blue Shoes

For one day, tried acting like Chuckie